IN THE TIME OF THE DINOSAURS

Millions and millions of years ago, there were no people in the world. There was summer, but no winter. And there were the strange animals we call the dinosaurs. Some of the dinosaurs were so big that they would have made our elephants look small. But others were no bigger than our chickens. Some dinosaurs ate plants, the way horses and cows do today. But some liked to feed on other dinosaurs. The dinosaurs were gone long before the coming of the first men. But the great bones they left behind tell us all about them and their strange world.

In the Time of the
DINOSAURS

By William Wise
Illustrated by Lewis Zacks

SCHOLASTIC

New York   Toronto   London   Auckland   Sydney

ISBN 0-590-41149-7

12 11 10 9 8 7 6 5 4 3 2 1   7   7 8 9/8 0 1 2/9

Printed in the U.S.A.   09

Millions and millions of years
ago, the world was very warm,
much warmer than it is now.

There was never any winter then.
There was never any snow.

Warm rain fell on the land. Even
the sea was warm.

In this warm world lived strange animals called dinosaurs. Some of them were the biggest animals that ever walked the land. They were the kings of the world for millions and millions of years.

In the days of the dinosaurs, there were no men. So no man has ever seen a living dinosaur.

But we know what kind of animals the dinosaurs were.

We know, because we have found their bones.

These bones have told us many things about the dinosaurs.

We know how the dinosaurs lived.

Some dinosaurs lived near the water.

Some dinosaurs lived away from the water, on dry land.

We know what the dinosaurs ate.

Some dinosaurs ate only plants, the way horses and cows eat grass now.

Some dinosaurs ate other animals, the way lions eat other animals now.

We know how large the dinosaurs were.

Some of them were bigger than any animal you have ever seen.

But some of them were as small as chickens.

The dinosaurs who liked the water lived near warm ponds.

Or they lived near warm, slow-moving rivers.

Many green plants grew there and the dinosaurs liked to eat them.

This was one of the first dinosaurs.

He was very big. His body was as big as a truck or a small airplane.

He had a very long neck. He had a very long tail. And he had a very long name.

His name was Brontosaurus (Bron-to-SAW-rus).

Brontosaurus lived near the water.

He ate leaves and bark from trees that grew by the shore.

Brontosaurus found much of his food near the water. And he needed a lot of food because he was so big.

Brontosaurus was big, but he was not safe. There was another dinosaur that wanted to eat him. This dinosaur was called Allosaurus (Al-lo-SAW-rus).

When Allosaurus came near, Brontosaurus ran away.

He ran through the mud.

He splashed through the water.

Allosaurus did not have long legs like Brontosaurus. Allosaurus could not follow Brontosaurus into the deep water.

When Brontosaurus got to the deep water, he was safe.

Some of the first dinosaurs were much smaller than Brontosaurus. They could run much faster.

This dinosaur was ten feet long. But he only stood as tall as a man. He was called Camptosaurus (Kamp-to-SAW-rus). He lived near the water, too.

When Allosaurus came, he ran away. He ran behind the trees. Or he ran quickly through the mud and the water if it wasn't very deep. Allosaurus, who sank into the mud, could not catch him there.

This dinosaur was called Ornitholestes (Orn-i-tho-LES-teez).

He was not very tall. He was about as tall as you are. He could run very fast. He could hide behind trees or plants because he was so small.

Some of the first dinosaurs did not live near the water.

One of these was Stegosaurus (Steg-o-SAW-rus). He lived on dry land and ate the plants there.

Stegosaurus was one of the first dinosaurs to have armor. He had armor plates on his back. You can see how the armor plates went from his head to his tail.

Stegosaurus had a tail that kept him safe. On the end of his tail there were four long spikes.

No other dinosaur wanted to get near those spikes.

Not even Allosaurus. So if he was not very, VERY hungry, Allosaurus left Stegosaurus alone.

Not all the dinosaurs lived at the same time.

Brontosaurus, and Allosaurus, and many other dinosaurs lived for millions and millions of years. Then, one by one, they died out.

Brontosaurus died out.
Allosaurus died out.
Stegosaurus died out, too.

But many new dinosaurs came to take their place.

This was one of the new dinosaurs.

He lived in the water, or near the water.

His name was Edmontosaurus (Ed-mon-to-SAW-rus).

Edmontosaurus was a big dinosaur. He was as tall as a tall tree.

He ate only plants and leaves.

Edmontosaurus had a long, wide tail. He could swim with the help of his tail.

Many of the new dinosaurs did
not live near the water. This
dinosaur lived on dry land.
He was called Struthiomimus
(Stroo-thee-o-MY-mus).

He had no teeth.

He ate plants and leaves and small animals.

To be safe, he had to run and hide.

Some of the new dinosaurs had armor to keep them safe.

This dinosaur was called Paleoscincus (Pale-e-o-SKINK-us). He ate plants and leaves. He had heavy armor on his back.

His tail had spikes on both sides.

No other dinosaur wanted to come near an animal with a tail like that.

Some of the new dinosaurs had horns.

This dinosaur had three horns.

He had a little horn on the end of his nose.

He had two big horns above his eyes.

His name was Triceratops (Try-SER-a-tops).

Triceratops was a big animal. He was much bigger than a horse or a cow. He had small teeth. He ate only plants and leaves.

But because of his horns, Triceratops was not afraid of any other animal. He was not even afraid of the most terrible dinosaur of all—Tyrannosaurus (Tye-ran-o-SAW-rus).

Tyrannosaurus was one of the last of the dinosaurs. He ate only other animals.

45

He stood twenty feet tall. He could look over the top of a tall tree.

From his nose to his tail he was almost fifty feet long. He was as long as a big truck.

His teeth were as long as a man's hand. And his mouth was full of teeth.

He was the most terrible animal that ever lived on the land.

When Tyrannosaurus came, the other dinosaurs ran.

Some ran into the water.

Some ran under plants or behind trees.

All the dinosaurs ran—all but one.

Triceratops did not run.

Triceratops stood right where he was.

He saw Tyrannosaurus. He saw the terrible teeth. But Triceratops was not afraid.

If Tyrannosaurus was looking for a fight, Triceratops would give him one.

Most times, Tyrannosaurus went away and left Triceratops alone.

There were other dinosaurs to catch and eat.

Other dinosaurs that were not as big as Triceratops.

Other dinosaurs that did not have two big horns.

But if Tyrannosaurus was very, VERY hungry, he stayed to fight. And what a terrible fight that must have been. The most terrible fight two animals ever had.

Many times Tyrannosaurus won.
Many times he was too strong for
Triceratops, but not always.

There were many times when
Triceratops won, too.

Triceratops must have been a
brave animal.

Any animal must have been
brave, to stay and fight with
Tyrannosaurus.

Then, after millions and millions of years, something happened to the dinosaurs. All at once, they began to die out. But this time, no new dinosaurs came to take their place.

Edmontosaurus died out.
Brave Triceratops died out.
Even Tyrannosaurus, the most
terrible animal that ever lived, died
out too. At last there was not one
dinosaur left in the whole world.

No one knows why all the
dinosaurs died out.

All we can do is guess what may
have happened.

We know that the world became a little colder. It was still warm, but not as warm as it had been before.

Maybe the dinosaurs could only live when it was very warm. And they died out when it grew a little colder.

No one knows for certain why the dinosaurs disappeared.

All we know is that the dinosaurs lived for millions and millions of years.

For millions and millions of years
they were the kings of the world.
Then they were gone.
And no animals like them have
ever been seen again.

Dinosaurs in This Book

Allosaurus (Al-lo-SAW-rus)

Brontosaurus (Bron-to-SAW-rus)

Camptosaurus (Kamp-to-SAW-rus)

Edmontosaurus (Ed-mon-to-SAW-rus)

Ornitholestes (Or-ni-tho-LES-teez)

Paleoscincus (Pale-e-o-SKINK-us)

Stegosaurus (Steg-o-SAW-rus)

Struthiomimus (Stroo-thee-o-MY-mus)

Triceratops (Try-SER-a-tops)

Tyrannosaurus (Tye-ran-o-SAW-rus)

Scientists have given some of the dinosaurs new names.

The new name for Brontosaurus is Apatosaurus (A-pat-a-SAW-rus).

The new name for Struthiomimus is Ornithomimus (Or-nith-o-MY-mus).

Tyrannosaurus is also known as Tyrannosaurus Rex. This name means "king of the tyrants."